Death by a Dream

Luke C Yourston

authorHOUSE®

AuthorHouse™ UK
1663 Liberty Drive
Bloomington, IN 47403 USA
www.authorhouse.co.uk
Phone: 0800.197.4150

Published by AuthorHouse 04/20/2018

ISBN: 978-1-5462-9203-6 (sc)
ISBN: 978-1-5462-9202-9 (e)

In a time, starting in New York City, where the people were festive and the lights shined pretty. A time where snow glistened the skies and music played throughout the night, lived an orphan girl. Who could only dream of what a real Christmas would be like but little did she know, she wasn't any ordinary girl. She was somewhat different and about to experience a different kind of world. This is a story that digs deep into your mind and leads you to another time, but I must warn you... This isn't for the faint hearted.... Now if you please, let's get started.

Flashback

Since Isabelle was at the age of 5, every Christmas she would sit up high on the window ledge, leering out of her frosty window wondering, wishing she could feel what it's like to sit by a flaming fire along with a hot cup of coco in hand topped with whirling whipped cream and as an accessory of the softest marshmellow that you could use as a pillow. a huge dazzling Christmas tree with the most ravishing decorations surrounded by a dozen Christmas presents wrapped so elegantly but piled up like a magical mess. The most important factor that she wants the most is a loving family, a mom, a dad maybe a brother or a few sisters to look up to or, be a role model to. She was dropped off at the orphanage 5 years ago at the age of three. She never really had any recollection of her parents, as she was too young to remember. She had always wondered why? Why did they give her up? Was there any reason? Alternatively, did they just not want her? These questions would spring to mind every now and then and suddenly dropped her mood crashing through the floor. Let's take you back 5 years ago, the day Isabelle got dropped off in a small cradle just outside the two gigantic doors of the orange. Her parents were at the time in a dangerous business. Her dad was a drug lord of a wealthy stature and her mother was his accomplice if

1

you like. Money to support Isabelle wasn't an issue. It was the constant violence taking place and constant moving of location, which put not only her parents in danger but also Isabelle herself. one particular day when an overcast of clouds were approaching from a distance white fluffy snow covered the pavements entirely, Isabelle was playing on her front lawn that was surrounded by a picket fence that stood at 4 foot tall Isabelle was with her dolls at the time minding her own business. a man dressed all in black, black leather boots up knee high a black leather jacket with thick black buttons buttoned up to his neck black trousers and dark shades of glasses. He stood still sibylline as the earth came to a stop. Just glaring with a stare that could kill, maybe that was his intentions. Her dad noticed him and kept a close eye on his precious daughter. He noticed this mysterious man reach in his pocket and pull out a gun. He then quickly yelled 'ISABELLE' he didn't waste no time he shot out of the front door and picked Isabelle up and turned his back to protect her from what was coming. Everything went silent for a moment he looked back and the mysterious man was gone. He then looked back at Isabelle and got down on one knee, the look upon his face was fearful, shocked, stunned with a worrying breathing pattern. her mother came rushing out with a towel wrapped around her head and her waist, soaking wet as she just got out of the shower 'what's up I heard screaming' her dad looked at her but said nothing, he picked Isabelle up and went indoors. 'she can't stay here, in this house or with us' her dad said Isabelle's mum looked at him then looked at Isabelle then began to reply 'what are you suggesting' he replied with a single word 'orphanage' so that's when they packed all of her belongings, clothes and toys and everything. Then placed her in a tiny cradle along with a few blankets to keep her warm from the battering winds and the ice like coldness that was rushing through the air on that evening. They hopped in their car and sped to the orphanage. They placed her on the porch with a note saying___

this is Isabella she's 5 years old and we are unable to take care of her due to personal circumstances, we've bagged all of her belongings in the bags laid next to her cradle, please take care of my special princess and sorry for any inconveniouns.

Then they drove back to their home and left little Isabelle at the orphanage. The oldish woman around 42 ms peacock who wore like a green knitted sweater red socks up knee high and a long blue skirt. As soon as she first noticed, Isabelle ran down a set of stairs, 6 steps to be exact. She looked left then right as cars were whizzing by and the rain was chucking it down, but she didn't see any sign or suspicious people who may have dropped Isabelle of. So the woman took Isabelle inside and cared for her ever since. Isabelle had three other roommates Andrea, Robyne and Nicklous, Robyne's story was different, she was never in any real danger, she came from a family of 7 a mother, a father, 4 brothers and a sister. Living in a single small terrace house. Living in poverty was the devastating part of their life is, struggling every day to survive, scraping and scrapping for food and money every day. Well one day Robyne snuck out of her house a minute after 12 while her siblings and parents were all sleeping. She would sneak out occasionally and go to a nearby park, just to use the swings and think. She was only 7 but at that time there was a lot of things to look back on and reflect on. She was swinging in the moonlight as a bright light shone down on her. Over in the distance she noticed something unusual lurking in the shadows. She hopped of her swing and went to investigate. As she approached this mysterious object, which looked like a huge tall man standing as a staunch brick wall blocking her path then instantaneously jerked forward and pushed Robyne over she, screamed "ahhhh" got up without hesitation and ran home with all possible haste. As she came upon her home, she espied smoke coming from her home she came to a sudden stop scandalized about what she's seeing. A huge explosion occurred moments later. Robyne screamed 'NOOOO' as she sniveled and sobbed. Her 17-year-old brother came running out of the house scorching in flames, go to the end of their drive then plummeted to the ground. No one else made it out. A few hours later all of her family were pronounced dead, her whole world came crashing down that's when a social worker came and took Robyne to an orphanage where she would finally meet Isabelle. at first they didn't talk for a few days, Isabelle would try to converse with her but Robyne was traumatized more than anything. Until finally she spoke up 'why are you here?'

'I don't know, I don't remember I've been here for as long as I can remember, what about you'

'I remember, remember witnessing my whole family burn to death right before my eyes while I was hopelessly watching from the side lines' Isabelle was stuck on words she slowly sat down on her neat cozy bed, 'I'm sorry' said sorrowfully. Andrea was more outgoing and extroverted, she was only the age of 6 when she got placed into an orphanage, Andrea and her family were on vacation in New York for

Christmas. It was her first time spent in this magical place, there were carolers, big bright lights, and big fat fake Santa Clauses ringing small convivial bells. They were all standing around a huge 20ft Christmas tree awaiting for the lights to light up. Then began a countdown '5, 4, 3, 2, 1' then the lights came on and everyone cheered in elation. A sparkle caught the corner of Andrea's eye and as curious, as she was she went after it. She went through and around everyone that was in the way. 'Time to go back to our motel room' said her mother then looked around but no sign of Andrea 'Todd! Todd!' (Andrea's dad) 'Where's Andrea?' Beginning to panic, Todd does a whole 360 turn looking for her and says in a worriedly tone 'I don't know' the sparkle that caught Andrea's eye led her to a dark ally away from everybody not a soul in sight, she looked down this dark eerie pathway and felt as if her entire body had been taken over something extremely possessive. At the end of this path stood a tall man, the same sort of man that was in Isabelle's and Robyne's story. This man, whose identity is secret started walking towards Robyne step by step he started picking up speed and go faster and faster until he was running towards Andrea, she took a step back but slipped on a rusty can on the ground and twittered her ankle, her father and mother seen Andrea on the floor so they went rushing over 'Andrea' they hollered Andrea looked at them and screamed 'help!' when she looked back this strange man was gone, like he had vanished without a trace. 'It's ok darling we're here' her dad picked her up and they went back to their motel room. They arrived at the motel they were staying on the 12th floor of this 20-story motel. So instead of using the stairs they were going to use the elevator. But the elevator was out of order. Todd went to the reception desk and asked 'why is the elevator down; the receptionist replied with 'I don't know, they've been out for a while' then the lights started oddly flickering but nothing was thought of it 'ok' they were forced to use the stairs which seemed like it would take forever and a day to climb. They finally reached the top and got into their hotel room. Her mother was desperate for the toilet so she went as soon as they got in. Andrea sat on her cushiony bed. Daunted by what she witnessed. Nothing was said for about 10 minutes. Her mother was still in the bathroom 'Amanda?' (Andrea's mum) 'what's taking so long' no answer so Todd went to investigate, he slightly opened this white awfully squeaking door and peeped his head around the corner but what he saw dropped his face as if he needed a top up on Botox. He saw Amanda laying fully clothed in the bathtub with the shower pipe wrapped tightly around her throat, blood gushing from her eyes, nose and running down her cheek. She wasn't moving she was still skin was cold like she had been laying in the snow for several hours. Todd rushed over to Amanda and tried to get the pipe removed from her throat the door then suddenly slammed shut making a huge BANG noise, which startled Andrea. Everything went quiet 'daddy' she said no answer she creeped up to the door, and again whispered 'daddy' no answer, she slowly opened the door with a nervous shake. She first noticed blood splatter all across the bright white tiles of the bathroom walls and she screamed the roof down 'ahhhh' he farther was lying in a pool of blood sprawled out with a gash in his head unconscious. Andrea stormed out of the room and flew down the flight of stairs and went to alert the reception of this devastating situation. Which by then is what caused Andrea to become an orphanage ms peacock (owner of the orphanage) took Andrea in and as luck happens Robyne and Isabelle was around the same age so she was paired up in the same room. The first time meeting Isabelle and Robyne she never socialized for about 3 whole days. After 3 days had passed. She opened up to Robyne and Isabelle, but what she came out with wasn't a usual conversation starter 'have you guys seen the man in all black' Isabelle and Robyne looked at each other this is something even they haven't discussed. Isabelle and Robyne chirped up simultaneously 'yes!' they frozen looks went whizzing around the room in confusion. The final child involved in these mysterious going on is 8 year old Nickolous. He was a rebellious young boy living with his mother, his farther left when he was merely a baby. Some would say that not having a farther figure around caused psychological issues and maybe this was the case for young Nickolous. One Christmas Eve Nickolous was watching the tv sat comfy in his black leather reclining chair, he overheard his mother on the phone which sounded like she was having an heated argument. 'NO, I don't want your money, leave me alone me and Nickolous don't need you in our lives' his mother was shouting aggressively 'was that dad again' her mother looked at him and only said 'why don't run to the shop and get yourself some sweets' so Nickolous jumped up out of his seat and ran to the shop, the shop stood on the corner of his street, it was only a stone throw away, he'd be quicker than the flash. 'ok mom' so he went into the damp air and glacial gust of winds. He finally made it to the shop he decided instead of getting sweets he wanted a drink to sooth his dry lips. He approached the fridge packed with a variety of refreshments that stood behind a thick pane of glass he opened the fridge went straight for the ribeena. He closed the fridge and seen a reflection of a very tall man with a black scarf covering his face and like a black cloak almost worn as a cape. He sharply turned around but nothing was behind him so he thought nothing of it, it could have possibly been a mirage that his mind was playing on him. So he paid for his drink and headed home. He opened his front door and said loudly 'mom I'm back' but she didn't answer he felt a chill, a draft coming from the kitchen and he went to investigate. The back door was wide open 'mom, are you outside' she still never answered and creped outside he then ran quickly as he noticed a deep hole in the garden as he approached he shone a torch down on the dark grass in which he stood on. The grass looked as if it was torn up, like someone was dragged through it. He shone his torch down this dark hole his face struck thunder with shock. His mother laying at the bottom with a slit throat eyes wide open and a vacant kind of look. Nickolous dropped to his knees and broke down in tears. That's when he had no choice but to go into the orphanage. The final member to a sinister escapade that awaits the young unfortunates. Each of them were emotionally scarred from what they've witnessed during their very short lived lives so far. Isabelle, Robyne and Andrea all went up to Nickolous who was sitting on a high window ledge watching the world go by athe time Isabelle began to converse 'hey Nickolous? Do you recollect seeing a tall man dressed in all black' Nickolous turned his head looking very confused. He thought to himself how? How do they know what I've seen. He replied 'yes, why?' the others just glanced at each other. 'We've all seen the same kind of figure, something strange is going on here' ms peacock burst through the door and startled the children especially Isabelle who gave of an abrupt gasp. Then sounded a sigh of relief. 'Right children time for bed, we've got a busy day tomorrow, the Christmas fair won't be around forever' she went and shut the curtains blocking out any kid of light from shining through. Then took the children in. they didn't have any intention of telling ms peacock about this mysterious man haunting them. 'Ok children, now get some sleep' then she switched the lights of and left closing their wooden creaking door behind her. As soon as she left, Nickolous pulled a touch out from under his bed, the same touch that he had kept since that night he witnessed his mother's lifeless dead body. 'Guys what's going on' he began to say. Isabelle replied 'I don't know but whatever is going on, its affecting us all' Robyne and Andrea agreed she continued to say 'and I reckon it has something to with this "man" he might be responsible for your parents death'

'But what about your parents, did they not get killed? Andrea questioned Isabella turned away got out of bed and opened the curtains to glaze out of the window then began to reply with 'I don't know if my parents are dead or alive, that still remains a question that keeps coming to mind' Robyne chirped up and said 'I think we better get to bed before ms peacock comes up and tells up of'

'yeah your right, Isabelle are you are coming?' she replied with a single word 'yeah' then they all got under the covers and went to sleep except Isabelle, who laid with her eyes wide open thinking. That's all that she could do, are her parents dead... or alive.

3.026 words.

This was only the beginning to a twisted plot, a beastly horror that cannot be stopped. The children were unaware that what's yet to come will be quite a scare. Something like a dream but can be considered as a nightmare.

2 Christmas fair

7am ms peacock rushed through the children's door and opened the curtains harshly. Letting in a beam of blinding light. 'Come on get up and out of bed, rise and shine got a busy yet exciting day today' the children woke groaning 'it's too early' Andrea said but without choice, they had to be up. So they got up brushed their teeth had a quick wash and got ready. Well everyone did apart from Andrea who fell back to sleep. so the others devised a plan, they decided to grab a corner each of Andrea's bed sheets in which she was laying. Then they flipped her up out of her bed crashing to the floor, they were all in hysterics apart from Andrea who had a mood on her and she stormed out of the room unpleased and raging. She came back into the room 15 minutes later still with a sour face 'oh cheer up' Nickolous said 'right children have you got all of your scarfs and hats and gloves on, its below freezing outside and the snow is piled up to your hips today' 'yeah i think we have everything' they said simultaneously and they went of wrapped up like a dogs dinner. they walked for about 10 minutes before getting to the fair. They eventually made it, the place was lit up, carousel rides, food stalls, and dazzling shops filled with toys surrounded covered in white glowing snow. 'Ok well here we are, you can go do whatever you like, just meet me back here in 5 hours'. So the children went off together. 'What ride shall we ride first' Andrea said Nickolous responded 'I'm not riding no rides besides, fairs creep me out'

'Ok, well Robyne, Isabelle fancy going on anything?'

'Yeah I'll go on something with you but only if it's not too scary or high like rides, i don't do heights.' Isabelle wasn't paying any attention to what was being said, her entire focus was all on this toy store over the way. Something was attracting her towards it something possessive, she glared and glared blocking out all clamor 'Isabelle...Isabelle' Andrea began to say Isabelle turned to look but appeared looking confused, like she was on a whole other planet. 'Huh' she uttered 'do... you... want... to go on a ride?'

'errrm no I'm alright' then continued to stare at the toy store. 'I'll catch you lot up later' Isabelle said the others agreed 'ok suit yourself, come on Robyne lets go on the ghoul of ghouls' enthusiastically said Andrea so they went of Nickolous shouted 'i'll just watch from the sidelines!' Isabelle didn't have any kind of notion to what was so fasinating about this particular shop. She peeped through the window and there stood a big brown bold teddy bear on display. She smiled as her eyes lit up. She also noticed a man in there, which sat at a wooden desk, which looked to be the shopkeeper. He wore a bow tie with a buttoned white t-shirt and black trousers he had short grey hair and a few wrinkles upon his face. She entered the shop and sounded the bell that was right above the door. She walked over the hard wooden floor to the teddy bear. And went to touch it but before she had a chance to the shop keeper placed his hand upon Isabelle's shoulder and startled her. 'Hi, can I help you' 'n n no I was just looking' she began to stutter. He just grinned ear to ear. 'Where are your parents?'

'I don't remember them I'm an orphan'

'Oh right, well in that case follow me I want to show you something' so they both went over to his desk and opened the middle draw and pulled out a necklace with a weird kind of pendulum attached to it, it was the colour of a bright green meadow and had three spear like points to it, with the middle point being the longest and the other two equal lengthen he looked at Isabelle then looked back at this object which was in his hand. pondering...... 'Hmmm, what's your name' he questioned 'Isabelle'

'Ok Isabelle this right here' holding the pendulum up swinging it right in front of her 'this is a special gift, it will help you in your desperate needs but only works around Christmas period. All you have to do is wear it round your neck and hold the strings while swinging it and say the magic words "be gone" that's all you have to say if you come into any real kind of danger, the creature or thing may not disappear completely but it will leave you alone like you don't exist.' Isabelle was amazed but she didn't quite believe it…She took the pendulum then questioned 'why do you say "creature" or "thing"' he looked confused, but responded with 'just an example' with a grin upon his face. Isabelle just nodded her head and looked down at the pendulum, it began to glow a bright green colour it was fascinating. 'now go have fun "be gone" the shopkeeper said jokingly, so Isabelle stood up and walked out of the shop as soon as she left the shop she took the pendulum and placed it around her neck and covered it up with her thick white fluffy coat and long black scarf, she didn't want the others to see what she had.... not yet anyway. Isabelle met up with others at a food stand. 'Oh hey Isabelle, where have you been' Nickolous said Isabelle replied 'just browsing round the shops' the others thought nothing of it as they bite down on their piping hot hotdogs. It soon was time for the children to meet up with ms peacock. 'Hey children, did you have fun?' ms peacock wondered. 'yesses, but Robyne did about poo her pants on the ghoul of ghouls' andrea said 'yeah it was so funny' laughed Nickolous. Robyne replied annoyed 'oh shut up! It was frightening'

'What about you Isabelle?'

'Yeah it was fun' Isabelle didn't go into too much detail, she wanted to keep her pendulum a secret from the others. Back at the orphanage around 10 o'clock, everyone was getting ready for bed. They all got their pjs on, well everyone apart from Isabelle. 'Isabelle? Why aren't you in your pjs' Nickolous questioned. Isabelle never answered him she got beneath her duvet and turned her back to the others. 'Are you ok?' asked Robyne.

'I'm fine!!' she said angrily 'just leave me to sleep, I'm exhausted' the others looked at each other, Nickolous just shrugged his shoulders and closed his eyes wanting to sleep. Eventually everyone fell to sleep. While Isabelle was only pretending to be asleep. She got up out of bed and snuck out of her room on her tiptoes trying not to wake the others she opened her door slowly as it was creaking so loudly like rotting floorboards. Then she made her way down the hall and to the bathroom. Where she locked the door behind her. She took her coat off along with her pendulum, which was given to her. She was studying it with her eyes looking at it up and down, as it was glowing green she went into a daze as if she couldn't take her eyes of it. Then a loud knock on the bathroom door which startled Isabelle and broke her from a trance. It was Andrea 'Isabelle hurry up I'm bursting for a wee' said while rubbing her tired eyes. So Isabelle quickly put her pendulum back on along with her coat then unlocked the bathroom door and walked straight past Andrea without saying a word, Andrea glared at Isabelle as she walked down the hall. She didn't think much of it so carried on to the toilet.

1.314

3 Bona fide

Isabelle woken but was freezing cold, shivering to the bone, hands, feet and her buttoned nose was numb. She opened her eyes to a frozen wasteland with a heavy blizzard slowly approaching. She stood up and did a whole 360 turn but nothing...she couldn't see anything for miles. Only open land covered by thick snow. She thought she was in a dream and everything she was feeling and seeing wasn't real. So she thought to herself if she tightly closes her eyes and counts to 3 she'll awake safely in the comfort of her own bed. That's what she did, Isabelle took a deep breath and exhaled. She closed her eyes and clenched her fists then began to count '1...2...3' and stood still for a few seconds before reopening her eyes. But nothing happened she was still stood in this impairing blizzard that was getting stronger and faster by the minute. Young Isabelle tried to stumble forwards to find some kind of shelter but the blizzard was proven too strong, her frail body couldn't handle it so she plummeted to the ground and curled into a ball hoping that it would pass soon. But that was very unlikely as it just kept coming. She began to give up hope as she laid frozen beginning to be buried by snow. In the distance, she saw a shadow of a man walking closer and closer towards her. All she could clearly see is big black boots and baggy long red trousers.

As he reached her, she tried to get a glimpse of his face but her vision was blurry, eventually she flaked out. This man took her to a big warehouse kind of building, decorated like a winter wonderland, bright lights, toys galore, a gingerbread houses built big enough for you to live in and a huge massive Christmas tree which stood in the middle of the floor topped with a dazzling star. Isabelle was still unconscious laying in a red king sized bed, she looked as though she was lost at sea. Tiny little men and woman in green bright suits with silly long hats gathered around her bed silently discussing her presence they have never had this happen before, they have never witnessed an actual child before. Isabelle woken up slowly opening her eyes, the first thing she seen was little faces that were around. She scuttled back in the bed frightened 'Where am I? Who are you?' then this man once again appeared 'you're quite alright child, don't be scared we won't hurt you, we'll help you if anything' then something in Isabelle's mind clicked... 'you're Santa' she said shocked, 'and your all of his elves' she heard a strange woman hollering 'saint nick, saint nick' she appeared and stopped in her tracks once she seen Isabelle, and glared at her 'what are you doing all the way out here' she questioned Isabelle stuttered 'I I I don't know myself, I woke up here' Santa and Mrs. Clause looked at each other confused Santa replied 'you couldn't have just woken up here, that's impossible isn't it'

'That's what I thought, but I think I'm just in a dream and I'm sure that I will wake up any time soon'

'Oh Isabelle this isn't no dream this is all real, and how you came to be here is beyond belief' Mrs. Clause said things went quiet for a moment. Then an eerie noise sounded outside like a screeching kind of noise and a gust of wind blew open all of the windows, everyone in Isabelle's room got down to the floor, the elves rushed over to the windows and shut them as quick as they could. 'what was that' Isabelle wondered but Santa quickly responded 'errrrm that was nothing just the wind howling and it seems as its getting stronger nothing to worry about' Isabelle didn't think anything of it, she stood up and walked over to the window to peer out of the window, she couldn't see much the snow was overwhelming but she did see that mysterious man again standing tall from across the way it startled Isabelle and she fell backwards and onto the floor 'Isabelle are you ok' Santa said as the elves went to help her up 'yeah I'm ok but there's this man that's be haunting me and I've just seen him again out there' she said quickly loosing her breath 'calm down Isabelle I'll take a look' Santa went over and looked through the window but nothing 'well whatever you saw is not there now, maybe you just need some rest' Isabelle was adamant in her mind that what she saw was not an illusion. she got back into her bed and just laid there staring at the ceiling. 'Ok Mrs. Clause, Timmy, Billy and Silly (the elves) we have work to do let's leave Isabelle to rest' so they went off and turned the lights off the room went pitch black then closed the door behind him. It wasn't too long before Isabelle fell asleep. The next morning she woke up but yet again, her mind must have been playing tricks on her. She opened her eyes to Andrea who was stood over her 'wake up it's nearly 12 o'clock' she said Isabelle woke confused she sat up and said 'how am I here' Andrea didn't know what to say she just gave her a funny look. 'no no no I was in a snowy wasteland about to freeze to death, then

Santa came to save me and bought me back to his workshop, I got to see his elves and Mrs. Clause and...' she suddenly stopped then continued to say 'I seen that man again'

'What man?'

'The one...The one that's been haunting us'

'Ok maybe it was just a dream...or a nightmare from the way you're talking about it' Robyne traipsed into the room 'what's going on in here'

'Isabelle is claiming she woke up in some other time and was in the presence of Santa and that'

'I'm not lying why won't any of you believe me' Isabelle frustratingly said she went to storm out of the room putting all force behind each stomp and barged pass Nicklous 'what's up with her'

Andrea replied 'she's just had a stupid dream' down a flight of stairs Isabelle flew down and shot out of the front door 'Isabelle Isabelle!' ms peacock was calling but it was too late Isabelle was already half way down the street sobbing her heart out. She came to an ally way and hid behind a dumpster leant against a brick wall slowly sliding down it in despair. Isabelle didn't know which way to turn so she whipped out her pendulum that was took into her coat and grasped it tightly with her hands looking down with an evil look upon her face, the look of the devil. There was no telling what was going through her mind. Back at the orphanage ms peacock was panicking getting ready to go out and look for Isabelle 'come on everyone get your stuff on we're going to go look for Isabelle' as they was about to head out Isabelle walked through the door 'oh my god Isabelle, are you ok' ms peacock said with relief. She got down to her level and held her with hands but Isabelle didn't say anything she simply just turned her head away she did respond. Eventually and said 'I just want to go to my room' ms peacock just agreed 'ok' and let her go 'Robyne, Nicklous and Andrea go keep an eye on her' and that's what they did they followed her up to her room. As each day went by Isabelle became more and more troubled. It was only a couple of days from Christmas and Isabelle hasn't been talkative since she ran away. They were all in their room laying down on their beds Isabelle finally spoke 'guys only a couple more days till Christmas' Nickolous replied with a shocked tone 'yeah it's exciting'

'Who knows it could be our last Christmas together' Isabelle said 'Isabelle? What do you mean?' as Isabelle continued to stare into space she said 'well no one knows the course of life anything could happen...here...or someplace else'. The rest of the children looked confused then laid down and began to fall to sleep.

This is it the part with the twist, the part that will leave you somewhere in the mist lost to possibly disappeared within. The horror that awaits these 4 children will leave you quaking on the edge of your seat held up in anticipation, waiting...but for what...your about to find out.

 # it begins

It was icy, freezing cold; snow was rising inches by the minute. The children all woke simultaneously they were frost bitten from head to toe. 'I told you I wasn't lying' Isabelle said Robyne, Nickolous and Andrea all stood up on their feet amazed by what they were seeing 'woooooe' they said 'but wait...doesn't anyone find it weird how we are all here together if this is a dream' Andrea said. The others just gazed at each other 'yeah it is a bit but we really need to find shelter this blizzard is getting stronger' a bright light caught Isabelle's eye 'hey look over there maybe there's shelter there, let's go so they went of this light that they was following could have been anything they was only heading into oblivion. They ran up a snowy mountain sinking into the snow struggling to reach the top Robyne slid down 'ahhh' she yelled but as quick as Nickolous was he caught her by the hand 'it's ok I've got you' he pulled her up and continued up the hill. They finally reached the top and seen the huge warehouse covered with decorations 'look over there that's where Santa is' Isabelle said 'how can you be so sure'

'Because I've been here before like I said' Isabelle replied. 'Well what are we waiting for lets go, if I stop out here any longer I'll become a frozen snowman' Nickolous hastily said.

So they went off as quickly as possible they got to the front door and tried to open it but it was strangely locked. With the children, shivering slowly becoming icicles they just had to find a way in so Robyne rushed around the side of this place and noticed that a side window was slightly open she tried to pries it open with her bare hands but Robyne just wasn't strong enough, the window was stiff from the ice around the ledge. She hollered over to the others 'hey guys there's a window here we can climb through but I can't open it'. They rushed round to the window, Nickolous seemed to be the strongest so he had a go to open it 'here let me try' he grabbed the bottom of the window and pulled as hard as he can, you could see the veins bulging in his neck and head, that's how desperate they was to get out of this storm. Finally, he managed to get it open by using every possible strength in his body. Andrea was the first one who hopped through the window followed by Isabelle and then Robyne then finally Nickolous. They were inside and out of the storm but still freezing cold, it would take a while before they warmed up unless they could find some kind of heat source, the place was pitch black not a single shine of light, it was nothing like what Isabelle previously saw. There wasn't any noise or anybody in sight the place looked like a dump. Something was odd. Isabelle went for a little stroll before she heard a crunch like sound; she looked down towards her feet and noticed a smashed picture frame. Isabelle bent down to pick it up. It was a picture of Mrs. Clause and Santa Clause together posing in front of that huge Christmas tree. She was confused to why this was just laying around on the floor. The place had looked like it had been abandoned, dust and cobwebs everywhere. 'Isabelle?

Is this how it was when you was last here' Andrea said she replied 'No...Nothing like this...but what was that light that lured us to this place? I don't see any light' they continued to look around. Something to Isabelle felt very strange. The floorboards in this spooky place were actually rotting, you could see mice running beneath their feet scattering. Robyne was squeamish as it is and she jumped up onto an old wooden chair sat in the corner covered with dust and cobwebs 'ahhhh' she screamed 'oh my god there's loads of them there all over the place'

'Oh get down, there only mice their harmless' Andrea spoke. 'No, no I don't like them' Robyne was screaming 'so what you gonna do stay up there forever'

'As long as the mice are there, then yes' Isabelle went wondering off, to explore this dreary place. She walked down a long corridor, pictures on the wall were crooked, there were shards of glass laying around all over the floor, like mirrors have been shattering for centuries. Isabelle had to mind her step if she didn't want to get slashed. Isabelle reached the end of the corridor, which lead to a wooden door; she looked at the door debating whether to go through or not. Then she decided what's the worst that could happen. She reached for the doorknob and held it tightly beginning to turn it clockwise as it screeched. Isabelle pushed the door open and she saw an old desk and an old rusty chair she looked confused. She wondered up to the desk and came across a note on the table with ink spilled across the page in which the note was written on. She picked up the note but couldn't quite make out what it says. She tried to squint her eyes and read the note but still couldn't quite make it out. She could only read single words, that didn't make no sense. It read.

_____evil   is   lurking_____whoever reads_____safety_____dead_____painful death_____ follows.

The door then slammed shut unexpectedly and unexplainably. It startled Isabelle she drops the note and rushes to the door and tries to open it but it just wouldn't budge so she starts screaming for help 'hellllp, somebody I'm locked in' the loud slam also startled the others that was still in the same room. However, they was unaware that Isabelle wasn't there. They was too focused on calming Robyne. 'Isabelle?' Nickolous called 'what was that noise?' Robyne whispered Andrea answered 'I don't know but we need to find Isabelle' so they rushed of down the corridor running shouting 'Isabelle! Isabelle! where are you?' They heard Isabelle banging like a maniac on the door at the end of the corridor. 'Hang on Isabelle we're coming' Nickolous shouted they got to the door and was trying to turn the door knob but it was stiff and wouldn't budge an inch. 'Isabelle stand back I'm gonna knock it down' so Nickolous started to shoulder barge the door he hit it once...nothing he hit it twice...it budged a little then the third time he knocked the door down and he went down with it. Andrea and Robyne went inside without hesitation but Isabelle was not to be seen...she was gone. This was strange the atmosphere suddenly became spooky. Where could have Isabelle vanished to? The room had no windows or any loophole it was simply just a box. The other 3 were looking very bewildered. 'What the hell is going on' Andrea said 'I don't know' replied Nickolous 'let's go see if the storm is clear'

'But what about Isabelle?'

'She clearly isn't here, staying here isn't going to help her, she could be dead for all we know' so Nickolous went back to the room in which they were previously and the other two followed. He peered out of the window 'the storms calming but wait...what's that?' Nickolous noticed a huge unusual man carrying from what he can see looks like a lifeless body. Then he realised... it was Isabelle. Nickolous rushed out of this place and into the cold air Andrea took a peep and screamed 'OH MY GOD!!' so Robyne and Andrea went outside to. 'Hey stop there' Nickolous was shouting but this "man" couldn't hear him over the howling wind. He took Isabelle into another well lit up place. But this place looked like it was well looked after like there was actually someone living there. Kind of like a log cabin with decorations from head to toe. Nickolous, Robyne and Andrea just stood at the top of the snowy hill looking down on this place amazed. Reindeers came swooping down over the children's head they ducked feeling the wind of the deer's as they blew past. They decided to go and investigate they rolled down the hill and ran up to the front door knocking loudly. The door screeched open and an middle aged lady was standing tall in the door way. The children paused and looked this woman up and down. 'Oh, hello children come in come in, it's freezing outside' she said so they went rushing in to escape the bitterness of the cold. 'Right this way children' they followed. This place on the inside looked like a well-designed palace. A huge room big enough you would think that that room was the only room in this magical place.

They walked past a giant Christmas tree surrounded by gigantic presents. Almost as big as the children themselves. This woman took them to a bedroom on the other side of the building. 'Right in there, of you go, I'll go get you some blankets and hot coco to warm you up' she said smiling. The children wondered in. At the edge of a king-sized bed was a man sat on a wooden chair. He was dressed in all red with knee high black boots and a long thick white fluffy beard. The children looked up at him amazed. 'How're you doing?' he questioned he children was struck on words. Isabelle who was laying in that bed spoke up 'hey! How did you get here' said with excitement. The others looked at Isabelle and ran straight towards her 'I guess these are your friends Isabelle?' 'Hey are you ok?' Nickolous asked Isabelle responded 'yeah I'm fine, do you guys have any idea who this is' referring to this strange man they looked confused then she went on to explain '...it's Santa Clause...you know saint nick "HO HO HO" it's really him' Nickolous and Robyne actually believed that this was the real Santa but didn't quite understand how they came to be here. Andrea didn't believe any of it and she made that quite clear. 'I don't believe it... it's impossible'

'Nothing is impossible Andrea, just think how is it possible that you're all here together?'

'well yeah but____' then Andrea clicked 'how do you know my name?' Before Santa could explain Mrs. Clause came walking into the room with warm velvety blanket 'here you go this should sort you out, I'll place your hot coco's on the chest of draws next to the bed, feel free and help yourself.' Andrea didn't take her eyes off of Santa she became suspicious and felt like something down the line was wrong, she knew that the others wouldn't see it her way so she had to get to the bottom of it yourself. Santa was also staring back at Andrea evilly. Something deviant was lurking in the air somewhere. Isabelle was just lying in bed thinking to herself while the others were enjoying their hot chocolate. She began to have flashbacks of when she was first in this place, she couldn't figure out of it was all real, a pigment of her imagination, a dream or a nightmare everything was confusing. Then she remembered seeing that man again the man dressed in all black, she looked up at the window and wondered. Could history be repeating itself or is she stuck in the same time zone, she got up out of bed and went over to the window. She peered through it and could see nothing but the snow that was blowing heavily at an angle. isabelle then thought nothing of it. as she was about to turn away a black shadow caught her eye. she stopped and looked directly at this object. it seemed as if it was getting closer then all of a sudden a huge blast of wind blew open the windows and knocked isabelle to the floor. it made everyone else duck for cover. 'quick get them windows shut' santa was screaming. the childen apart from isabelle who was still on the floor in shock. rushed over to shut the windows. they had to use all of their strength because the wind was pushing against them. they finally got them shut then sounded a sigh of releife then fell to the floor exhausted. 'what the hell was that' robyne panickly said. isabelle was still struck by what she had saw but kept quiet. nobody still knew about the pendulum around isabelles neck this whole time she had refused to take of her coat. 'isabelle are you ok' santa said. she replied while staring of into space 'yeah i'm fine' then stood to her feet and wondered over to her bed and laid there all quiet.

'well come on you lot let's let isabelle rest' so they all left the room. andrea "desperatly" needed the toilet 'where are your toilets' she asked 'right down the hall and the third door on your left' santa said but as andrea was about to head to the toilet santa grasped hold of her arm tightly and strictly told her 'whatever you do don't go through the door that has a hook shaped handle to it' andrea looked frightened santa let her go. as andrea was walking down the hall she passes the door with the hooked shaped handle she stopped and glanced at the door debating whether she should investigate or not. But she didn't bother so she carried on walking...well that was until she heard music coming from that very room. As rebellious as Andrea was she just had to check it out. She reached for the handle and opened the door, the door creaked open. On the other side was a staircase, there was no telling of how far down it went because you couldn't see the bottom. It felt as if it lead to hell or an even more demonic place. But the curiosity was killing her, she was suspicious as it is. So she went ahead and began to walk down the staircase. she took three steps down then the door slammed behind her, she quickly around and misplaced her step and missed the next step down, she tripped and plummeted all the way down the steps, grazing her knees and bashing her body against the solid stone steps. She crashed at the bottom, after banging her head, she was barely conscious. Her vision was blurry. Andrea couldn't make it to her feet. But she could hear classical music coming from a room opposite to where she had landed. As she looked down the narrow hall to this room. She could faintly see shadows moving swiftly. Andrea tried to get up but as she made it to her feet she fell back down. Her legs were severely damaged...Possibly broken. Andrea used her head and thought to crawl her way down the hall. so that's what she did she slowly crawled laying on her abdominal and using her arms to pull her broken body closer to the door. Andrea finally approached the door covered in sweat from the effort it took to make it. she peeped around the corner and what she saw was horrifying, shocking, disturbing...... something she would have never have guessed in a million years. She seen dead lifeless bodies hanging from the ceiling by nothing but steel chains and hooks. There was also a man, dressed in a black coat, black scarf and black trousers, he was dancing with the cadavers, like he was having a good time, a party like this was all normal to him. Then he would place the cadavers on an operation table and chop of their heads, then drain their blood and store it in bottles. It looked as if they were for his consumption. He tossed their heads into a shredder making mincemeat out of them. Andrea was almost sick she kept heaving she just couldn't help it. Andrea made that much noise this strange man heard her and stopped what he was doing immediately. He turned around and noticed Andrea on the floor just outside the door he picked up a knife and rushed over towards her Andrea tried to scuffle back but he was too fast. He grabbed the door and opened it aggressively. Then grabbed Andrea by the hair and dragged her to the table, he knocked the cadaver that was previously on the table of and onto the floor. Andrea was kicking and screaming begging 'ahhhh!! please please please don't hurt me!!' he carried on like he couldn't hear her and slammed her down on her back and tied her down by a thick steel chain. Andrea was painfully crying looking up to the ceiling as tears rolled down her face. He took the knife that he held in his hand and put it up to Andrea's neck getting ready to cut it off but unlike the others that were dead...Andrea would be alive.

 **strange going on's**

Back up in the main hall Nickolous and Robyne was waiting for Andrea to get back from the toilets but it felt like they was waiting for Christmas. 'Isn't Andrea back yet?' Santa questioned 'no she's been gone for quite a while I'm gonna go look for her' Robyne replied 'ok, be careful' Santa said Nickolous thought that it was strange how Santa said "be careful" what could possibly happen. Robyne went off down the hall that had a long shiny red carpet spread across the floor stretched out all the way down the hall and plant pots that was as tall as her. This was nothing like what Andrea seen on her way down the hall, maybe they were in the same time but trapped in a different world. As Robyne was about to pass that door with the "hooked handle" she also heard classical music. She was curious but she just carried on walking minding her own business. She passed a few more doors and right before she reached the bathroom Mrs. Clause popped up out of nowhere 'hey Robyne what are you up to' she scared the living day light out of her she was finding it hard to catch her breath. Then she came to say 'I am looking for Andrea, have you seen her?' heavily said. She replied 'No I can't say I have. A huge smashing sound came from Isabelles room Nickolous ran quickly and knocked the door through and stopped looking around the room feeling an awful draft, Robyne rushed back down the hall and came up behind Nickolous and was also in shock Isabelle was...gone and the window had been smashed. There was no glass on the inside though so whatever or whoever smashed it did it from the inside. Santa and Mrs. Clause came barging through 'WHAT THE HELL HAS HAPPENED HERE!!' Santa was screaming. Nickolous began to stutter 'I I I have no idea' but before Santa could reply Nickolous ran of outside, the storm had calmed down but the wind was freezing cold his strands of hair stood up on end as soon as the air hit his pale skin. Robyne followed. 'Nickolous wait up'

'What!' he shouted Robyne gave him a vacant look 'what's up?.

'What isn't up? Why are we even here? What's going on? I feel like I'm losing my mind' he said while hyperventilating then slid down the side of the log cabin till he was sitting then placed his hands in his hand weeping he was. Robyne bent down to his level and put her hand on his back to comfort him 'it's going to be alright, I'm sure it's all just a dream'

'But what if it isn't what if it's all real' Robyne sat down beside him and started to think then she seen that man gain from across the distance she began to say 'Nickolous look there's that man again' and pointed in his direction Nickolous looked up but..... he didn't see anything 'what man'

'Over there can't you see him!' beginning to get frustrated Robyne stood up and ran towards that man to confront him. On approach she stood face to face. The man had his thick black hood up a dark balaclava and shades on so Robyne was unaware of who it is. Her breathing pattern began to get heavier and heavier. This man started to remove his shades and took his hood down then removed his balaclava. Robyne gasped and stumbled backwards fell into the snow, which laid beneath her. She began to stutter "I I I thought you was dead?" He just smiled his eyes began to squint as he looked down upon Robyne she continued to say "I seen you burn to death right before my eyes. The explosion the horror no one survive.... H H How is this possible" he stood over her looking down he began to say 'how do you live with yourself?' Robyne replied 'what are you on about?' he smiled 'seeing your own brother burn to death right before your eyes as you just stood there helpless'

'I was in shock it was too late the damage had been done'

'No no no no, if you didn't sneak out you would be dead too, that's why I'm here...to kill you' then he reached into his black cloak and pulled out a machete and held it high above his head. As he was about to swing down on Robyne, she put up her hand and tuned her head away still laying down hopeless on the ground. 'Robyne? Robyne?' Nickolous yelled over Robyne's brother stopped in his tracks and looked up. robyne raised her head and he was gone... Nickolous seen Robyne laying on the floor and rushed over to her aid 'hey what you doing on the floor' he lifted her up and Robyne broke down in tears and then wrapped her arms around Nickolous and squeezed him tightly. Nickolous didn't anticipate this so he asked her 'are you ok?' and put his arms around her. 'What happened'

'My dead brother I seen my dead brother'

'That's good right?'

'It would've been apart from him trying to kill me'

Nickolous didn't know what to say he was struck for words. 'Really? ok let's get back to Santa's place maybe he knows what's going on... come on' they headed back Santa was waiting at the door for them, 'back so soon are we, what's up with Robyne' he said 'she's had a nasty shock'

'Oh my, really what happened?'

'her dead brother tried to kill her' Santa glared at Nickolous and then turned to Robyne 'that's not possible' he then stormed out of the room and went down the hall way until he came to that door with the hooked shaped handle and looked at it, as if it wasn't there like he could see straight past it. He reached to open it. Mrs. Clause came running over to him 'wait don't open it' Santa replied 'I have to before...something terrible happens' so he opened it and went down the staircase and down the hall. He burst through the door but...no body was even there. There was blood everywhere splattered up the walls over the operation table, all over the floor like a slaughterhouse. Santa muttered to himself 'I'm too late'.

Where was Andrea, is she alive...is she dead? Nobody knew. Robyne was so shaken up, it was like she wasn't there, nothing but a hollow shell staring into a dark abyss. She was wrapped in a pink blanket sitting upon a leather sofa. Nickolous was sat merely a meter away from Robyne. Just glaring at her. He was concerned. Santa came back after disappearing for quite a while and sat beside Nickolous then began to say 'will your friend be alright' Nickolous replied without taking his eyes of Robyne 'I don't know' at this moment everyone was silent still shallow breathing, waiting for a sign, waiting for something to happen, just waiting for the oblivion. 'And Andrea...what about her, where is she at' Nicklolous said hoping for an answer. Santa looked at Nickolous and then turned away without saying a single word 'there's something you're not telling me, isn't there?' Nickolous knew that something wasn't as it seemed. Santa decided to stand up and walked away but Nickolous wanted to get to the bottom of it and stood up and chased after him 'what is it that you're not telling me!!' he was yelling. Santa walked down the corridor and went to the door where Andrea first went missing. 'Through this door' Santa said Nickolous looked very confused 'what's through that door'

'Andrea went through that door' Santa opened it fully and Nickolous looked upon a starecase after a brief second he flew down the steps and barged through the door at the bottom. The first thing he seen was bodied dangling from the ceiling, blood splatted across the walls and all over the floor and the operation table. Along with a machete placed on the table. The first thing that sprung to mind is Andrea is dead. He began running round the room checking all of the bodies hoping and praying that one of them isn't Andrea. Santa soon came tracing in. He looked directly at Nickolous sorrowfully and Nickolous looked directly at him like he could kill his eyes were filling up with water his hands were two balled fists. Emotions were running high. He took a glance at a meat cleaver laying on the side, and he went to pick it up. He held it up to Santa and demanded some answers 'you know something and you're not telling me!' Santa looked at Nickolous with his head held high and walked around the room. 'Yes I know what's going on... I don't know where andrea is exactly but she should be dead' Nickolous paused he froze in time he dropped the meat cleaver and fell to his knees dazed and slightly in shock.

His ears began burning from the words that he was hearing. Santa began explaining 'you see Andrea, you and Robyne all play the victims, you all have a past where you could have saved a life…. a life that mattered. But you did nothing, nothing at all!!' Nickolous stood back up on his own two feet and said 'my mother died because of unfortunate events that had nothing to do with me' Santa quickly replied 'she was still alive Nickolous!! But you wouldn't have known because you never checked, did you? You could have saved her life. Has anyone ever told you, "don't believe something unless you know for certain" that's the story with you' Nickolous began thinking then maybe he was right in what he was saying he felt light headed a little short of breath kind of upset and frustrated with himself then he said 'but what about isabelle, you haven't mentioned her at all'

'Now Isabelle is the victim, she's the one who lost her life to a point where they couldn't save her'

'So why is she here with us' Santa laughed while smiling uncontrollably 'she's the reason why you are here, she's the one that's planned it all to teach people like you who take family for granted'. As soon as Santa finished explaining he barged past Santa and ran up the steps as quickly as his legs would take him and back to the main room yelling 'Robyne, Robyne we've got to go and get out of here' he got to the main room and Robyne was tied to a chair gagged, hands tied and a thick rope wrapped around her body so she could barely move, there was also a cloaked person standing behind her.

the reveal

A voice came from the shadows 'where are you going to go, after all this is all in your head...and Andreas head and Robyne's head...even my head. tThen she came out from the shadows, Isabelle appeared dressed in all black like the rest of them. She even had her pendulum on but this time she wasn't hiding it and it was glowing violently green. Nickolous stopped in his tracks and glared around the room 'Isabelle what's that around your neck' she smirked and replied 'just something that Santa gave me when I visited his toy shop'. Then Santa reappeared Nickolous felt trapped he felt cornered there was nowhere to run or hide 'where's Andrea?' he questioned Isabelle replied 'apparently she got away, but she can't be far we'll get her' Nickolous couldn't believe in what he was seeing let alone hearing. He thought he could trust Isabelle but it just goes to show that even your closest friends you can't even trust. He thought he knew her but in reality he didn't know anything about her. He couldn't think straight his mind had left his body his brain had shut down he felt weak, somewhat paralyzed. As he was taking tiny steps backwards, he bumped into something. Another cloaked person. Who it was he had no idea until, she revealed herself. His heart sank tears came running down his cheek like burst water pipes. It was his mum. She stood over him and glazed down in disgust she didn't say a word. She looked around the room catching a glimpse of her surroundings. Noticing a sharp shard of glass on the floor from the broken window previously. She walked towards it and picked it up then went back to Nickolous. Nickolous quickly stood up and started to explain himself almost begging 'Mum please don't I was scared, I thought you was dead I'm sorry I didn't have the intuitive to actually check to see if you was still breathing, now I know the truth I deeply regret it mum please I'm sorry' tears were flooding the room. But it was like his mum wasn't listening she kept on walking towards him. Raising this shard of glass going to violently stab him to death. The others were just watching. Robyne was kicking and screaming trying to call for help but there was nobody there to help. Besides her mouth was taped shut so to call for help would be impossible. Isabelle watched with a smirk upon her face he demonic plan was working splendidly. Nickolous backed up as far as he could go he hit a dull red wall, hoping he was going to see another day. But things weren't looking up. He squinted his eyes tightly and turned his head hoping for the best. Then a brick comes flying through a window and crashes to the ground everyone looks round to see what had gone off. That is when Nickolous took the opportunity of diversion and ran towards Robyne. He quickly untied her and ran out of the door with her. They see someone waving at the top of this snowy hill. At a closer look it was Andrea and they soon ran towards her without hesitation. Isabelle ran to the front door and watched as they escaped. She grinned as if she knew this was coming...so what is Isabelle's next move?

odd turn around

Nickolous, Andrea and Robyne had been running through the ice cold snow for about fifteen minutes hoping to get away from Isabelle and those "things" they knew they were their family but they didn't really exist. They were exhausted but luck happens, Andrea notices a log cabin over in the distance. But the others don't see it. 'Over there the log cabin we can go hide out in there'

'What log cabin?' Nickolous questioned 'I only see a run down house, if we enter that it's liable to come down on us' but as well Robyne again sees something totally different from the other two. 'All I see is a factory, something like of willy wonka' but needless to say they still ran towards whatever it was that awaited them in the yonder. They arrived. 'I still don't see much of a log cabin'. Nickolous nervously said Robyne agreed 'yeah me either I don't' even see a run down house' then they exchanged looks of fear towards each other Andrea went to walk through the front door 'wait Andrea what are you doing' he shouted andrea replied 'going inside it's freezing out here' Nickolous paused 'but the front door is over there' andrea looked confused and went inside. To Nickolous and Robyne, Andrea disappeared vanished. 'Andrea!!' they both were shouting, she then reappeared 'how did you do that' Robyne said 'Andrea replied 'do what'

'Walk through walls' Andrea had no idea what they were talking about. Nickolous went over to the door that he could see he grabbed the handle and went straight in. He then vanished and Andrea witnessed it she looked shocked, amazed by what she saw. 'You just disappeared right then' she said, 'what's going on here' worrying Robyne then it came to Nickolous 'to me it seems like we're all in a separate dream or nightmare whatever this is, but in a different world, place in time a different atmosphere. We're seeing differently yet we're in this together' Robyne nearly fainted 'so does that mean when we go into these buildings, which aren't the same buildings in which we all see. we'll be on our own' Robyne cleverly asked Nickolous looked at them both and said 'it looks that way' the atmosphere felt like the world was about to end, or a huge chunk out of their world was about to disappeared...... forever. Nickolous began to say 'well we can't stop out here we'll freeze to death' then took a silent break. 'Looks like this is it, this is where we split and...who knows what's awaiting for us just round the corner.' Emotions were running high Robyne had crystal clear tears running slowly down her face. She walked up to her door and took a glace back before...shutting it to. Andrea looked directly at Nickolous and spoke 'good luck, hopefully we'll get out of this and go back to our normal lives' Nickolous nodded. Andrea walked to her door and waved goodbye then...closed her door. Nickolous was left alone, he never thought that he would hear how peaceful the world (or this world that he undeniably is trapped in) could be. He looked over the smooth mountains paved with snow took a deep breath and walked through his door.

Andrea

It was dark, pitch black. Like time had no existence. Andrea was uncertain of this...place that she was in. Weary of her surroundings, as she's already experienced anything can happen. It seemed like a normal log cabin, there was a warm fireplace with a fire blazing giving of the only light in the room. A deer's head mantled up on the wall. And the smell, was indescribable it wasn't bad unbearable like dead rotting flesh but it wasn't a good fragrant smell like a scented candle waring away the wax. As Andrea began to walk, the floorboards beneath her feet began to creek unearthly to what the ear is used to. She was looking around not knowing what to expect, she came across a shelf screwed deeply up onto the wall. And noticed a picture. The picture was covered in dust she could not quite see it so she blew the dust of. Which tickled a sneeze and she sneezed dropping the picture that she held in her hand. The picture cracked as it crashed to ground. She bent down pick it up and sighed in annoyance. She glanced at the picture then dropped it again. However, this time on purpose she was in shock she took a few paces backwards and fell onto a chair. The picture was when she was a kid along with her mother and father. A family portrait. She thought how? This can't be why would a picture of her and her parents be in this place when they have never stepped foot in a log cabin before especially this particular one. She got up and ran into the next room slamming the door behind her. She stood in a hunched motion looking down to the floor legs spread apart a few inches and both hands on the door barely holding her up. Andrea turned around but it was dark, she couldn't see a thing. Andrea slowly began to walk forward while sliding her small hands along the wall hoping to find a light switch of some kind. She came across a square box like shape on the wall (click) the whole room lit up. It was almost a replica of the last room she was in but...this one had a weird feeling to it. 'Hello' Andrea was saying she moved around cautiously. The door that she previous came from opened sharply and smacked the wall. Another cloaked being came rushing through. Andrea began to panic and screaming 'help, help' but there wasn't anyone else around. She ran to another door located in the corner of the room and ran towards it as quickly as she could she ran through it and bumped into someone else of bigger physique. She stopped and looked directly up at them. Then the one that was chasing her spoke in a soft voice 'Andrea' Andrea turned around and replied 'mum' then she removed her hood and revealed herself Andrea burst into tears so much her vision became blurred. Andrea turned around and wept while she said 'dad' he then removed his hood and looked at her despised. He brushed past Andrea and stood by her mother. 'you two are dead, I saw you right before my eyes' as her parents looked down on her, her dad reached inside his robe and pulled out a sharp pointy knife. Andrea took a few steps back and gasped heavily. 'You know, Andrea I don't want to do this but...I have no choice' her dad began to say in his low-pitched manly voice. Andrea looked at him gone out at this point she was very confused to why they was doing it. 'If you don't want to do this then why are you? You don't have to' she replied practically begging Andrea's mum spoke. 'It's Isabelle, she's the one doing this she's controlling us, with that green pendulum that swings from her neck, you could have saved us that night, but you didn't, Isabelle didn't have a chance with her parents but you did, that's why she's doing this.' Andrea stumbled her words 'b b b I how could I have saved you, it all happened so fast'

'If you didn't go chasing that "thing" or whatever it was you could have altered the entire universe, none of this would be happening...that's how you could have saved us' Andrea's dad mentioned then Andrea began thinking, maybe her dad was right, maybe it was all true. She turned her back to them ashamed to look at them; her eyes were welling up with tears. She can't go back and change anything what is done, is done. Her dad walked up behind her and grabbed her hair and wrapped it around his hand and dragged her to the floor almost detaching her hair from her scalp. Andrea was screaming in agony. Her mum then stomped on her hands and feet breaking bones as she did it. There was no way that Andrea could move at this point let alone walk. Her dad grabbed her by the scruff of her neck and held a knife to her throat slowly grazing the cold jagged steel across it. 'I'm sorry Andrea...we love you' then he sharply slit her throat and allowed her to bleed to death as her body was jumping on the floor. The whole room was silent Andrea's mum and dad stood over her watching as she laid in a pool of blood. Andrea...was dead. Her parents left the room and headed outside slamming the door shut behind them.

 # Robyne

Robyne has entered a large factory, this place seemed like it's active. She was surrounded by large machinery. Saws, wielding equipment, conveyer belts the lot. As she walked around the room, inspecting her surroundings she placed her hand on a machine that looked like it was to saw right through ice. As curious as Robyne was she couldn't help but touch the blade so that's what she did she leant over and went to touch it, without a second to think she quickly moved her hand and held it tightly because the blade was scorching hot. Robyne then knew that these equipment's are used regularly and often. She knew that she wasn't alone. She began her search around this huge place. She came to a flight of stairs. As Robyne looked up them she got awful butterflies ten to a dozen rushing through her making her feel like they was scratching and clawing her insides taring away the flesh trying to see the day of light. With no exaggeration, it was safe to say that Robyne was terrified. Robyne closed her eyes and took a deep breath before commencing to climb the cold steel steps. She made it to the top and was awaited by a manikin in a pose that looked like they was frightened of something but what remained the question, but it seemed strange. Why was a manikin in a place like this it just doesn't make sense. Anyhow Robyne didn't think much of it and she walked right past it and continued her search. Music began playing from this room a few feet from Robyne, a door was slightly open too and a light inside was flickering like a bug zapper when a bug comes into contact with it but not quite as intense. Robyne slowly approached the room and pushed the door open a little just enough so she could peep her head inside. The room was empty, bare like nothing compared to the other rooms that was packed with stuff roof high, there was a music box laying in the corner of the room that was placed on a small table, she entered the room and went to switch the music box off. Standing there staring at the box thinking to herself why or how is this here, even more why is it on. She turned round and her brother was right there stood by the door, with a baseball bat in his hand, He stood with his shoulders back stiff as a board staring Robyne down. He wasn't happy at all, he frowned looking like he was about to attack Robyne before explaining why. Robyne still didn't know why he wanted to kill her, she was clueless. Was she going to get an explanation? She begged for one. 'Please tell me why you're doing this, please I beg you' he replied 'it's not me, you've got to believe me I don't want to, but I have to' this made no sense to Robyne what so ever 'if you don't want to then why!' she said getting heavily angry. He stepped inside the room and slammed the door. Robyne stumbled back and knocked the music box onto the ground crashing. Without another thought, he took a swing at Robyne but luckily Roubyne got out of the way and his bat went crashing through the table snapping it in half. Robyne rushed out of the room and down the stairs heading towards the front door but...the front door no longer existed. This worried Robyne so much that she began getting the nervous shakes. Her brother shouted down to her 'there's no escape Robyne, Isabelle thinks you need to pay, so this has to happen, whether you like it or not' Robyne blocked out what he was saying, she believed that there is always a way out of any situation, so she began to look for one and wasn't about to give up. Her brother began walking down the steps, allowing the bat to clash with the steel railings making an awful racket (ting ting ting) he started shouting 'Robyne you're only delaying the inevitable.' Robyne began panicking even more she noticed a small rectangular window, it was too high for her to climb, so she began to look for a stool or chair that she could possibly use to levitate her body up and through the window. A chair was sat beside her that she didn't notice before so she rushed to grab it and placed it directly beneath the window. She scurried up and tried to open up the window but it was stuck. She pulled and pulled the handle until it snapped! She fell plummeted to the ground and badly injured her shoulder. Her brother walked up to her and stood over her with that aluminum bat held in his hand. 'You don't have to do this'

'I have no choice, it has to happen, I don't want to but... it's just the way it is.'

'Please...no' Robyne practically begging. Robyne laid helpless and battered. Her brother raised his bat above his head high and swung down, connecting with Robyne's skull and cracking it open, crushing her cranium. He repeatedly hit her in the same spot until her brain was oozing out mushy like a can of dog food. His silver aluminum bat now was a crimson red colour. He had a tear running down his cheek, But he had to do it...so he believed. He left her there... dead to the world.

10 Nickolous

In Nickolous's mind he envisioned a rundown house. What appeared on the outside is exactly how he pictured it would be on the inside. Rundown, that's what it was. Everything was grey and black like an old pictured film. Rats scattered past Nickolous's feet in a hurry and escaped through the cracks in the floorboards. The roof looked as if it was about to collapse at any moment, Nickolous knew it as well and it put him on edge. As he moved across the room he was making ever such a racket with every step, it was loud enough to wake the dead at a slumber party. He heard a loud moan but didn't know where it was coming from. He looked all around even did a whole 360 turn around but it went silent again. He crept over towards the charcoal ridden fireplace then he heard it again, that moan, it sounded like a woman. Nickolous placed his foot on this eroded piece of flooring and nearly fell through it. He just managed to save himself. He took a look down and realised that it lead to another room, a basement maybe. The drop was at least 10 foot. Nickolous knew he couldn't jump down without damaging himself. There have to have been something that he could use to hoist him down. Took a glance over to the fireplace and noticed a piece of long wire. He went straight over to it and picked it up so he could wrap it around his waist. He next need to find something to tie it to, as luck happens a wooden pillar stood tall in the middle of the room, although it didn't look stable so at first Nickolous was skeptical about the idea but it was the only idea that he had so he went for it. He tied it as tight as he could not allowing the wood to breath. He stood above the hole took a deep breath and jumped. Nickolous plummeted straight the bottom, the piece of wire was proven to be too small and as it reached the end of the line the pillar that it was attached to was too weak to support Nickolous therefore it snapped in half and the whole house came crumbling on top of Nickolous. A couple of hours later he awoke up after being knocked unconscious by the timber that bludgeoned him in the head. His vision was blurry but still managed to get to his feet still stumbling like he's been out all night drinking. Over in the yonder he seen someone walking up to him with a long knife. They came right up to him with bad intentions. Nickoulous was too delusional to realise what was taking place. Then stab. The person stabbed him in the gut as he fell to knees he looked up, his mum removed her hood. While shallow breathing he said 'why?' before she could answer he fell face first and hit his head of a plank of wood. Was he dead? Like him and his mother, her mother never made sure he was dead, as she dragged his body away through the snow leaving a pure red trail of blood.

Isabelle

Back at Santa's workshop, Isabelle stood chatting to Santa. Glazing through a window. Awaiting for results. She wanted them all dead in cold blood. 'What's taking them so long' Isabelle frustratingly said. 'They'll be back soon' Santa chirped up. Then out of nowhere, over the hill top Isabelle sees Andrea's mum and dad and she began grinning from cheek to cheek. Yet there was no Andrea her smile soon dropped as fast as it was lifted. 'Where's andrea!!' she was shouting. Isabelle stormed to the front door and opened it to greet Andrea's parents she began yelling 'Well? Where is she?' her dad replied 'we did as you asked, she's dead'

'I wanted to see her dead, so I know for certain' Andrea's mum said 'you can believe us, we slit her throat, Andrea is now merely a lost soul'

'But that's not what I asked!!' Isabelle reaches into her coat and pulls out her green glowing pendulum and holds it up, she says in a loud assertive voice, 'be gone, be gone' without any notice Andrea's parents evaporated into dust, blending into the snow. Santa watched back from the window smirking. Isabelle went marching back to the workshop and slammed the door while screaming the place down. 'She's dead Isabelle, you got exactly what you wanted' Santa had to say to calm her down. Isabelle began to calm, she walked over a large chair fit for a king and sat down, patiently waiting. Around 20 minutes later, the door opened swiftly and Robyne was threw straight through it, dead. Covered in blood from head to toe making it look like she had no flesh whatsoever. Isabelle gave an evil grin. She walked up to Robyne and kicked her as hard as she possible could. Robyne never even flinched...She was certainly dead for sure, which is what Isabelle wanted. Isabelle walked up to her brother and said 'I no longer need your assistance' her brother looked so confused like he was trying to get his head around an extremely difficult puzzle. Isabelle whipped out her green pendulum and said 'be gone, be gone' Robyne's brother began evaporating right in front of her eyes, as he was fading away he had the chance to say 'but I did exactly how you asked' Isabelle replied 'yes you did and I am grateful for that but as I said, you're useless to me now'

'Ahhhh' he was screaming. He was nothing but dust Isabelle picked up a dust pan and brush and swept him up, then lightly blew him away out of the window. The wind took him, where to? Where ever the wind dies down. Now she was awaiting her finally victim. It wasn't long before Nickolouse's mum shown up at the door with Nickolous laying unconscious. Like she did with Robyne she ran and kicked Nickolous in the guts but.... he murmured. Isabelle's face dropped a thousand feet and looked directly at his mum. Her soul's attention turned towards her and she began walking towards her with a slow motion. She want to reach for her pendulum but before she had the chance. 2 figures appeared at the door. They entered the room Isabelle had no idea to what was going. She stopped in her tracks. These people were hooded and had dark sunglasses so there was no telling who they were. The male spoke 'Isabelle why are you doing this' Isabelle was somewhat stuck for words, she was trying to get her head around it. Isabelle totally bypassed their question and replied with another question 'who are you' then the female removed all of her headgear and responded 'we're your parents. Her dad also removed his headgear. Anger was building inside of Isabelle she had her fists clenched and was looking at them as if she was wearing glasses and peering over the top of them. 'I'm doing this because of you two!!' She snatched the knife out of Nickolou's mums hand and charged towards her parents, with the sharp blade pointing towards them and she stabbed her mum in the gut, she plummeted to the floor in agony. Isabelle then ripped the blade out of her mother and stood over her looking down like queen. Her farther bent down to see to his wife; she was bleeding quite heavily and was going into shock. Isabelle's dad said 'we didn't abandon you because we don't love you, we did it to protect you' as tears were running down his cheek. Isabelle was past caring, she only cared about herself at this point. Isabelle wasn't Isabelle anymore, she was possessed, a demon that only knows how to wreak havoc. She took the knife and slit her own father's throat and left him to bleed out. While her focus was on her parents. She looked back and Nickolous was gone. She screamed at the top of his lungs 'where is he!!!' Suddenly Isabelle came short of breath, she felt a sharp prick around her lower back area, she glanced down and the end of a knife was peeping it's head out. Blood was dripping from her to the floor and she fell to knees dazed. Nickolous had a limp and he limped around to the front of Isabelle. He looked at her as if looks could kill. Isabelle began laughing but why? 'you can't kill me as long as I'm wearing this pendulum' she glanced up at him and finished her sentence 'I'm immortal' Nickolous totally forgot about Santa, Santa grabbed Nickolous by his jumper and hung him up on a coat hanger. 'Help put me down' he was saying kicking and screaming. Isabelle rose to her feet and pulled the knife from out of her back. Walked over to Nickolous and whispered into his ear 'you're gonna watch your mother get turned to dust' She turned to his mum and took her pendulum and said 'be gone, be gone' Nickolous began screaming 'NOOOO, NOOOO!' as his mother vanished. Nickolous was sobbing his heart out under his own breath he said to himself 'I'm sorry mum, I love you' and looked down to the floor in regret. Isabelle took the knife and stabbed Nickoulous repeatedly, over and over again until he was merely a carcass used as decoration. Mrs. Clause came into the room unaware of what's been taking place. She looked at Santa and then at Isabelle. Isabelle said to Mrs. Clause 'it's all done, now we just have to wait for our next victims. She sat in her chair, put her fingers together and began waiting... patiently. I pity any soul trapped in this time.

12 New Beginning

'Jimmy look out!' a girl shouted. A snowball flew across the school playground and SMACK hit Jimmy square in the face. Jimmy plummeted to the floor from the impact he wasn't moving for a second. The girl that warned him ran over to him, she started screaming 'ahhhh somebody get the nurse' blood was running down the side of his face. The snowball that hit him had a small rock encrusted in the soft snow. But was big enough to cause serious damage. It turns out that the rock had caused a nasty gash on the side of Jimmy's skull, causing him to almost bleed to death. A dozen of people were around gossiping amongst one another. Jimmy was barely conscious, he could hear his surroundings, but just couldn't move whatsoever. A nurse came barging through the crowd to assist Jimmy. 'Alright jimmy, can you hear me? Raise our right arm if you can' without hesitation he raised his right arm. 'That's good' the nurse said the bell rang to indicate the end of break. 'Don't you lot have classes to attend' she said assertively. Everyone who witnesses this incident soon scurried away. The nurse used her adequate skills and bandaged Jimmy's head up tightly to stop the bleeding and prevent infection then phoned an ambulance. 'It's gonna be ok Jimmy' this girl said 'are you Jimmy's friend?' responded the nurse 'No,

I mean I know him but I don't really talk to him, but I don't think it's right what those jerks did' the nurse looked at her 'what's your name?' she asked 'it's Blair'

'Ok Blair do you know the names of the people who did this to Jimmy' Blair responded 'Yeah I do'

'You're gonna have to give details to the police, in the worst case possible, which I hope it doesn't come to, they could treat this as manslaughter' Blair gasped hoping that young Jimmy was going to be alright. Sirens sounded over in the yonder they seen bright flashing lights speeding towards them. They pulled up fast and attended to jimmy. 'What's happened' the paramedic said 'he's been hit by a rock and has a massive gash in the side of his head' the paramedics got the stretcher out and strapped Jimmy to it then loaded him into the ambulance. Blair asked if she could go with Jimmy to the hospital. The paramedics asked 'are you any relation?' Blair replied 'no...But I am a close friend' the paramedic sighed and said 'yeah ok then' Blair hopped into the back with him and they slammed the doors shut and sped off to the hospital. One of the paramedics exchanged looks with Blair, he began to say 'he's gonna be ok' Blair looked at Jimmy with despondency. Arriving at the hospital 10 minutes later. The paramedics rushed Jimmy to his room where they would begin to sort his problem out. 'I'm sorry but you're gonna have to wait in the waiting room, no one's allowed in while surgery is taking place' One of the surgeons said to Blair and Blair left to wait patiently in the waiting room. About 3 hours later, which seemed to be forever Blair was greeted by an assistant of the surgery. 'Blair?'

'Yes' she replied 'Jimmy is now conscious and if you wish you may see him now' Blair nodded and followed the assistant to his room. She entered to see Jimmy laying still, wide awake looking to the ceiling. 'I'll leave you to alone' the assistant said. Blair approached Jimmy and said 'how're you feeling?' Jimmy looked at Blair but didn't respond to her question. He instead replied with 'who are you?' things weren't as they seemed Blair responded by saying 'I'm here to correct your mistakes' as she walked around his bed side she confessed 'it was me who threw that snowball, and I knew it had a rock inside it, I want you dead...Jimmy.' Jimmy went into a panic and reached for his buzzer to alert the nurses and surgeons but Blair got hold of it first and threw it across the room. Which made a loud thudded noise. A nurse that was walking by heard the crash and stopped. 'Also my name is not Blair...it's Isabelle' The nurse walked in and seen Jimmy panicking so she ran to comfort him 'Jimmy what's up?' Jimmy was lost for words unable to speak. Maybe this was Isabelle's plan, this was a new beginning, this was her next victim, along with anyone else who deserves to meet death.

Wherever there is an end, there is a new beginning; sometimes it is a new start or a start of a journey to death. One day a world that we once knew will eventually lead to having nothing left.

Printed in the United States
By Bookmasters